To Peg Kirkpatrick
— N. W.

To Ramona Dane
with all my love
— B. M.

NANCY WILLARD

BEAUTY
AND
THE BEAST

Wood engravings by Barry Moser

Harcourt Brace Jovanovich, Publishers

San Diego   New York   London

HBJ

Text copyright © 1992 by Nancy Willard
Illustrations copyright © 1992 by Barry Moser

Library of Congress Cataloging-in-Publication Data
Willard, Nancy.
Beauty and the beast/by Nancy Willard;
illustrations by Barry Moser.
p.   cm.
Summary: Through her great capacity to love,
a kind and beautiful young woman releases a handsome young man
from the spell which has made him into an ugly beast.
ISBN 0-15-206052-9
[1. Fairy tales. 2. Folklore — France.] I. Moser, Barry, ill.
II. Title.
PZ8.W655Be   1992
398.2 — dc20   91-28398

A B C D E

BEAUTY AND THE BEAST

ONG AGO, when the century was still young, a rich merchant lived with his three daughters in a splendid townhouse in New York. The house looked out on Central Park on Fifth Avenue at Fifty-ninth, and the merchant had filled the rooms with treasures from his travels — tapestries and candelabra, chests and cameos, marble angels and bronze beasts.

In the evening, when lights blazed in every window, men in white waistcoats and women a-glitter with jewels were ushered into the dining room, where a long dinner table covered with gold damask and gold china and the finest crystal awaited them. Behind every high-backed chair stood a footman. And beyond the French doors lay the greenhouses and gardens. The merchant favored orchids and roses.

His daughters had a governess who taught them French and a maid who picked up after them and mended their velvet cloaks and silk gowns. When they wished to go visiting, the fat coachman hitched up their sleek horse, Blackett, and *clip-clop! clip-clop!* down the avenue sped their carriage to mingle with the other carriages of great families.

In the winter, the coachman took them for sleigh rides in the park. The cook served hot chocolate at midday, in a silver pot embossed with dragons. The butler lit a fire in the sitting room after supper and told them ghost stories, and his hands cast the shadows of men and women dancing, bearing trays, and lighting lamps. And the flames in the fireplace leapt, as if they, too, had a story to tell.

The merchant's daughters missed their mother, but only in a distant sort of way, for she had been dead a great while, and even while she lived she seemed not of this world. She had dabbled in magic and spent a great deal of her time studying the influence of the stars on her children and the healing powers of herbs on herself. From her father she had inherited a cabinet of rare books and a cottage in the country and a map for finding it, which showed it to be seventy miles north of New York City. She often went there by train, sometimes in the company of an elderly woman who called herself an astrologer. Neither the merchant nor Beauty and her sisters had ever been there as the place had neither gaslights nor running water, servants nor society—except the astrologer. Beauty knew nothing about the woman except that she had a great appetite for lemon tarts.

"I packed their lunch," said the cook, "and your mother always

ordered two dozen. And she didn't even like lemon tarts. So I suppose the greedy astrologer ate them all. Your poor mother!"

After her death, her gowns and her cabinet of rare books were taken to the attic and placed in a lacquered chest, across which a skilled artisan had carved a procession of stars and roses. On rainy days, Beauty fetched a lamp and crept up to the attic and opened the chest, and while rain drummed on the roof, Beauty tried on her mother's gowns and read her mother's books, which were mostly collections of fairy tales and treatises on gardening.

Her mother had asked the astrologer to name the children. The astrologer suggested Vanity, Money, and Beauty, and warned the merchant that if the children were given other names, bad fortune would plague the whole family. The merchant did not care a rap for astrologers, but he cared very much about names. The two oldest girls were named Vanessa and Mona. Beauty was christened Beauty, just to be on the safe side.

As Beauty grew up, everyone could see the name suited her, though her sisters' blue eyes and black hair were in vogue, and Beauty's green eyes and red hair were not. She'd learned a smattering of French from her governesses, she played the piano well and the violin badly, she could sing "The Last Rose of Summer" without losing the tune, and she was an excellent dancer. The merchant had sent his daughters to Mr. Dodsworth's dancing classes, where children of the best families learned the Viennese waltz, the grand march, and good manners. She could play chess. She could beat the butler because he let her win, and she could not beat her father because he did not. She loved the roses in her father's garden;

the maps on the walls in her father's study; stories that began "once upon a time"; walks in Central Park; and all animals, including bats.

"When I grow up, I shall run a hospital for animals," said Beauty.

When you met her, she remembered your name, and when you spoke to her, she listened. Pretty girls are a dime a dozen. Beauty is much rarer than you might suppose.

The merchant sent his daughters to boarding schools in Switzerland, where he hoped they would meet a lord or a duke or a prince. Princess Vanessa, Lady Mona — what a grand sound it makes in your mouth if your great-grandfather was a farmer in Connecticut! Vanessa and Mona loved being with a hundred other girls as rich as themselves, though they disliked wearing uniforms instead of pretty clothes. Beauty felt the skirt was much too long, and she would have shortened it above her knees if there hadn't been a rule against it. She hated the rules and the schedules that kept every minute of her day planned, for she loved to read, and there was never enough time to curl up in one of the leather wing chairs in the school library or on the bench in the adjoining courtyard with its lion's-head fountain and green glazed pots of roses. Very soon she had read every book on the library shelves, except the etiquette books, which outnumbered all the others and discussed matters in which Beauty had no interest: how to bow to the queen, what to say when you meet the Prince of Wales.

When the girls turned sixteen, seventeen, and eighteen, their father sent for them. Never mind that they'd met no lords and dukes, there were plenty of eligible young men in New York.

Luncheons at Delmonico's, dinners on the yacht, clambakes at Newport, and finally, a masquerade ball at the Waldorf-Astoria. Vanessa planned to come as Mary, Queen of Scots and ordered a gold embroidered gown trimmed with rubies and pearls. Mona fell in love with a gold-plated suit of armor; she would come as Joan of Arc.

"And who will you come as, Beauty?" asked her father.

"I shall come as a fairy godmother," said Beauty, "and I've found the perfect costume in that old trunk in the attic."

She put on her mother's best ballgown to show them and looked so like that long-vanished lady that the butler turned as pale as if he'd seen her ghost. Her sisters made fun of Beauty.

"Silly!" cried Vanessa. "Nobody will know who you're supposed to be! Who knows what a fairy godmother looks like?"

"I do," said the butler.

"So do I," said the cook.

"Me, too," said the coachman.

"I mean, nobody important," Vanessa corrected herself.

But a week before the great event, the merchant received word that three of his ships were lost in a storm off the coast of Newfoundland. Who can predict disaster? He called his daughters into his study and told them the worst.

"My dears, we are ruined. All this" — and he waved his arms — "must be sold. The yacht, the house in Newport, everything. We are moving to the country."

Mona and Vanessa were speechless.

"Where will we go, Father?" asked Beauty.

"We still have the cottage your mother inherited, near Elmore's Corners."

"And where is Elmore's Corners?" asked Beauty.

Her father showed them the great map of the Hudson Valley that hung in his study, and he pointed to a speck floating in a vast space high up along the river. Vanessa burst into tears.

"I shall try to find work there," said the merchant.

Mona announced that she would not leave the city — why, the social season was just starting.

"Everything we love is here," she exclaimed. "What shall we do for eligible young men? Do you want us to marry farmers?"

Vanessa said she knew plenty of eligible young men eager to marry *her*, though not one of them had yet got up the courage to ask.

But when word got around that the merchant had lost his fortune, the young men called no more. The butler, the cook, the coachman, and the maids were summoned to the merchant's study and given notice.

"No more hot chocolate!" moaned Mona. "Life isn't worth living."

Beauty thought she could do without hot chocolate, but not to hear the butler's ghost stories was almost more than she could bear. The butler shook hands with Mona and Vanessa and hugged Beauty.

"You'll visit us, won't you?" she asked anxiously.

"Oh, yes, Miss."

But his eyes said, *Now that your daddy isn't paying me, I don't have time for stories.*

She was amazed to discover how quickly three movers emptied their rooms, stripping away all traces of their lives. Marble angels, bronze beasts, gold china, tapestries, cameos were sold. Everything, everything. Even the books — all except those that had belonged to the merchant's wife. These Beauty begged to keep, along with the carved chest of her mother's dresses. Her father agreed. He knew these would not fetch much money.

On a warm Sunday in October, the merchant hitched up Blackett to their carriage, which Beauty had packed with pots and pans and clothes and blankets and smoked hams and hot-water bottles, and drove to the docks and stood among the mules and horses, the bales of hay and the men who loaded them. Across the Hudson unfolded the wide green countryside. Mona took one look and complained of a pain in her side.

"That's because you wanted to carry the smoked hams yourself," said Beauty. "There's plenty of space on the carriage."

"And plenty of people to steal from us," exclaimed Mona. "No thanks."

Vanessa was reaching into the carriage, tugging at something near the bottom of the load.

"I shall carry my hatboxes just to be on the safe side," she murmured.

Beauty glanced around at the mules, the horses, the bales of hay, and the men loading them.

"I'm sure nobody here has any use for your hats, Vanessa," she said. *And you won't either,* she thought, but she did not say this out loud.

During the crossing, Beauty stayed by the carriage among the beasts of burden, holding Blackett's reins in one hand while she worked the crossword puzzle from the newspaper with a gold pen she had borrowed from Mona and forgotten to return.

They all felt ill after the boat ride and were glad to climb into the carriage again. Beyond acres of corn stubble and haystacks rising in harvested fields, the farmhouses looked no bigger than teapots. Maples washed the air with a warm honeyed light and lit up the road like torches. The day was as ripe and inviting as a golden apple.

"How beautiful everything is!" exclaimed Beauty.

"If you can't say something sensible," snapped Mona, "be quiet."

The road narrowed into a stony path that led through the woods away from the river. It was early evening when they saw, far off in a small clearing, a low weathered house.

"Oh, no," cried Vanessa.

"Don't worry. We're not going to live in the chicken coop, silly," said Mona.

"Mona is right," said the merchant. "This can't be the place. Your mother always spoke of the cottage as white."

"That was years ago, Papa," said Beauty quietly. "Time passes."

And she pointed to the map.

When they pushed open the door (the lock was broken), Vanessa went in first, holding her nose. The house was damp and smelled musty. Light filtering through the dusty panes of the tiny

window barely lit the main room. A spiderweb ensnared Mona's ear, and she gave a shriek.

"I won't go in! I'd rather die than live in such a place."

Beauty followed her father into the other rooms.

One ladder led to a loft, which was dark and drafty, and another ladder led to the cellar, which held nothing but a shelf of milk pans. A rat peeked out at them and scurried away. There was a cupboard but no dishes, and a table and two oil lamps and two benches and an apple crate with OUR FINEST written on it that had been pressed into service as a stool. A teakettle hung from a crane in the fireplace.

"Thank goodness we didn't sell the blankets and dishes," said Beauty.

Ah, how lovely it would be to tell the maid to clean up the mess and find it done.

The merchant was pleased to discover a barn.

"It's odd what pleases us when our fortunes change," he observed, as he unhitched Blackett.

Mona and Vanessa volunteered to unpack the carriage. Beauty made up mattresses for herself and her sisters in the loft and a bed for her father downstairs by the fireplace.

"Let's see how hard they are," said Mona. She lay down on hers, Vanessa did the same, and the merchant thought he might take a rest, too. Beauty lay down for a nap because everybody else was doing it, and soon the whole family had fallen asleep.

The next morning Beauty woke first. She was famished, for they'd eaten no dinner the night before, so she crept down to the kitchen and cut herself a slice of the ham. The sunlight falling through the open door cheered her.

"I shall have a look around the place," she said to a spider, who was busy spinning curtains for the kitchen window.

Beauty was glad to find an apple orchard loaded with apples and a well nearby with a flat rock, on which rested a bucket and dipper. When she led Blackett out of the barn, she discovered an old wagon. The sight of their carriage next to this rough piece of work saddened her, but only for a moment. Behind the barn grew raspberries and wintergreen and the traces of a vegetable garden near a tumbledown woodshed, half full of old logs and kindling.

"I can start a fire with these," she said to herself, picking up a handful of small sticks.

She tethered Blackett to a post in the yard, filled the bucket at the spring, and carried water for the teakettle to the house — how heavy it was! — and fetched matches from their luggage. Tiptoeing around her father's bed, she soon had the fire lit. The fireplace did not draw well, and the lamps smoked; their crowns were crusted with soot. Her father sat up and groaned, "I'm so stiff I can hardly move," and Mona called down from the loft, "Is something burning?" and Vanessa said, "Breakfast, probably."

When the family sat down to cold tea and cold ham, Mona couldn't help saying, "How I'd love a cup of chocolate from our silver pot," and Vanessa remarked, "Beauty, what a wonderful farmer's wife you'll make."

"Oh, it's nothing, really," said Beauty. "You can be as good as I am, if you work at it."

And she made up her mind to keep Mona's gold pen.

The first day in their new home, Mona and Vanessa did not go outside.

"What is there to do outside?" asked Vanessa.

The merchant found it was no use nagging them to do chores. As the weeks passed, they rose at noon, put on their long skirts and whalebone corsets and high collars and their plumed hats, and moped around the fire on rainy days or sat in the yard on sunny ones and talked about the smart carriages on Fifth Avenue, the lunches at Delmonico's. Sometimes they took the carriage into town and stopped at the post office in the general store, for what is the use of putting on your plumed hats and high collars if there's nobody to admire them?

"Better to be admired by stupid folks than not noticed at all," said Vanessa.

Beauty had almost forgotten what it felt like to wear plumed hats and whalebone collars, and though the hard work tired her, she was glad to be free of rules and appointments. "If the headmistress could only see me now," she thought. She swept the house, washed the milk pans, filled them with milk, and set them out for the cream to rise, churned the butter, and scrubbed their linens on the rocks by the stream. She picked huckleberries and saw a bear that wagged its head from side to side like a stubborn child. She canned the huckleberries and made crab-apple jelly and wintergreen candy, which her sisters traded at the general store in Elmore's Corners for salt pork and cheese and fresh milk, and oats for Blackett.

Then the merchant caught a cold, which turned into flu,

which turned into pneumonia. In his delirium, he mumbled about his ships. Sometimes he said, "They're lost, all hands down," and sometimes he said, "I see one, I see one," and once he said, "Beauty, I dreamed all three came safe into harbor." The fever kept him in bed so many weeks that even Mona and Vanessa admitted he would never be really strong again. They agreed to do the cooking and the housework if Beauty would do the outside chores and chase off the bears and bobcats and check the fish traps their father had made and take care of Blackett.

"I don't know the first thing about horses," whined Vanessa. "Not the first thing."

Beauty took Blackett to the blacksmith for shoeing and cleaned the straw bedding from his stall and applied the currycomb to his coat, which was growing thick for the winter. The work tired her, but she loved the outdoors, and her father remarked that she had never looked healthier in her life. Evenings she read her mother's books or drew the apple crate up to the table, and her father drew up the bench that sat before the fire, and they played chess.

Every morning the merchant drove the wagon to the landing and met the mailboat from New York. No letters arrived for him. In the evening he counted the twinkling lamps on the barges and canal boats headed for Albany, and he listened to the slush of paddles from the steamers and faint music drifting across the water from the occasional sloop or schooner. He longed for his yacht, his friends at the Piccadilly Club, his top hat, and his overcoat with the fur collar. How, he wondered, could Beauty keep so cheerful? He would find her gathering chestnuts and crimson leaves of sumac to make into bouquets while her sisters sat by the fire and mended their lace collars. She traded a jar of her crab-apple jelly at the general store for a bag of daffodil bulbs and planted them all around the house.

"Remember those nights at the opera? What fun we had, sitting in Papa's box," sighed Mona.

"Remember the little elevator at Huyler's that brought fresh taffy every half hour?" said Vanessa.

Winter came early and fast. The earth turned hard and bare, the trees gave up their gold and hunkered down under a sky of frozen iron against which spruces and pines sent up dark spikes, and the bare sycamores shone bone white. An ice field stilled the river. The mailboat arrived, and the merchant heard news of a boat bound for Troy that rammed into the ice and sank into the dark, still water; he thought of his own lost ships. He watched the dark figures of the ice cutters scraping and sawing, loading the crystal blocks on the elevator and ramp that would haul them to the icehouse.

Suddenly the captain called his name and handed him a letter, his first since they'd left New York. The merchant's fingers shook so with excitement that he could scarcely open it, and he read it twice before he dared to believe the good news. The manager of his bank was writing to inform him that of the three ships he thought were lost, one had arrived safe in New York, with a full cargo.

What rejoicing there was around the hearth in the little cottage that night! The merchant was his old self again, lively and cheerful.

"What presents would you girls like me to bring you?"

"When we go back into society," said Mona, "no one must know we have ever been poor. I want that emerald necklace and diamond tiara I saw in Tiffany's before we left. If somebody's bought them, I'll settle for ruby ones."

"I'd like a green velvet coat lined with Russian sable," said Vanessa, "like the one you were going to buy me before we got poor."

An odd smile played over the merchant's face, but he nodded and turned to his youngest daughter.

"Beauty, what can I bring back for you?"

"I hate jewels," said Beauty. "You know how I lose things."

"A new dress?" suggested her father.

"It would get dirty so fast," said Beauty. "You know I spill jam on everything I own."

"There must be something you want," exclaimed Mona.

"A rose," said Beauty.

"A rose?" exclaimed Vanessa.

"That's what I want," said Beauty. "A rose. I haven't seen one for ages. I wonder if they still exist?"

Her sisters hooted with laughter, but her father said, "If Beauty wants a rose, a rose she shall have."

ARLY THE NEXT MORN-
ing the merchant led Blackett out of the barn, and Beauty packed
the saddlebags with fresh bread and cheese. Footprints leading to
the well across the snow startled her, and she was very much surprised to find Vanessa filling their father's flask with water. The
sisters stood in the road and waved to him till he rode out of sight.
The air was so cold that the ice cutters had not worked for two days.

Never had the merchant seen the world so still, the snow so
fresh and bright, embroidered with the tracks of birds and beasts
whose habits Beauty was just beginning to teach him. The snow
buntings were eating the frozen apples in the old orchard, and the
woodpecker, an early riser, was already hammering at the dead
sycamore.

The merchant rode across the frozen river at Hyde Park, left
Blackett with the stationmaster, and took the train into New York.
As he gazed out the window at the Hudson, he thought that his
wife might have ridden this very train long ago, and though she had
not entered his thoughts for many years, he imagined her sitting
beside him. He wanted to ask her if she, too, had heard the woodpecker in the forest, or at least its great-grandfather.

When he left the train and walked out into the street, the throng of carriages, the glow of lights in the shops, and the glitter of the city dazzled him and almost made him ill.

"I have lived too long in the country," he told himself and looked for a place to sit down. But there were no places, only the bustle of well-dressed men and women carrying parcels and getting in and out of cabs. As he strolled down Fifth Avenue, he tipped his hat to a few of his friends from better times, but they did not speak to him, and he was ashamed to speak to them. "All this will change soon," he assured himself. Suddenly he recognized the window of Tiffany's. He hurried inside, his spirits lifted.

The emerald necklace and diamond tiara were still in the showcase, and when the merchant told the manager that one of his ships had come in, the manager congratulated him and said how very glad all of them at Tiffany's were to see him, and of course he could have the necklace and tiara on credit.

"I'll have them delivered," said the merchant.

Two shops down, the green velvet coat lined with Russian sable had not been sold yet, either, and the merchant arranged to have it sent. The young woman who wrote out the order smiled at him and said, "It's your lucky day, sir. This morning two women came very close to buying this coat, and one promised to come back with her husband before closing time."

The merchant reached the docks at last and hurried into the main shipping office, emboldened by the thought that he would soon have the luxury of a carriage with a footman again.

The clerk behind the desk was polite but vague. Yes, the merchant's ship had come in, but her cargo had already been sold, and he could not say exactly what happened to the money.

"And now she is bound for the Cape of Good Hope," added the clerk.

"Do you think I'll go away just like that?" roared the merchant, snapping his fingers. "I'll settle with you in court, sir."

"Oh, will you?" sneered the clerk. "You'd better find yourself a good lawyer. And believe me, a good lawyer is going to cost you something."

Trembling with rage, the merchant turned and fled. He did not have even enough money to stay in the cheapest inn and barely enough to pay for his return ticket home. From the train he saw that snow was swirling against the glass. By the time the train dropped him off at Hyde Park, it was dark. The stationmaster, swathed in mufflers, met him with a lantern.

"I've come for my horse," said the merchant, and he put a coin into the stationmaster's mittened hand, which instantly closed over it.

"He's just where you left him," said the stationmaster. "I hope you're not thinking of riding him in this weather."

The merchant said nothing.

"Did you come from across the river?" asked the stationmaster.

"I did," said the merchant. "What of it?"

"Why, see here, s'pose your horse slips on the ice and breaks a leg. Where will you be then?"

"My horse is very surefooted," said the merchant and swung himself into the saddle. "Good-bye."

He could not admit that he'd hoped to buy himself a warm coat on this trip, and now he didn't even have enough money to spend the night in town. A raw wind shrieked across the broad field of ice as the merchant guided Blackett through the trees and onto the frozen river. Cold seared his face, and every part of him was chilled. Three feet ahead of him, the world vanished into the snow.

When the ice fields turned into a snowy path under Blackett's hooves, the merchant knew they had reached the other side of the river. Snow scarfed the trees, the hills, the road; still he could see nothing. The road to Elmore's Corners was not far off, if only he could find it.

Hsssss! The woods rang with what sounded like gunfire. Under the weight of the snow, trees were breaking. Blackett shied away from the path, terrified, as a large branch crashed at his feet.

"Let me not die in the forest," the merchant cried out, "never to see my daughters again."

No sooner had he spoken these words than he spied far ahead of him a light, and he plunged toward it. Behind him the blizzard howled and swirled, but ahead of him the air shone clear, and he was surprised to find the trees untouched by the storm. As the road wound through the woods, the air grew warm and tranquil, just as on that October day when he had set out for the country with his three daughters. It seemed to the merchant he was traveling backward in time.

The road burst into a clearing, and the merchant gave a cry of

astonishment. Before him rose the grandest house he had ever seen. It was much larger than his mansion on Fifth Avenue. Candles danced in every window, set with stained glass. The rooms seemed inhabited by emerald griffins and diamond basilisks, all going about their brilliant business.

Dropping the reins, the merchant climbed down from his horse and stumbled up the broad steps of the veranda. The front door was dark and plain, save for a large knocker in the shape of a winged snake. *Bang bang bang!* The merchant rapped it as hard as he could and prepared a little speech for the butler who would open it.

But to his surprise, the door opened by itself. Seeing no one, the merchant stepped inside. The smell of an excellent dinner overcame him, and he followed his nose. As he passed through room after room, his amazement grew. Each room seemed charged with the invisible presence of some loving soul who had lit candles in the sconces and fires in the fireplaces and moved on, leaving behind a fragrance of cloves and roses.

In all his travels, the merchant had never seen rarities to compare with what the rooms contained. In one he found a cabinet of ivory centaurs that danced in a circle when he bent to admire them. Another held a chair carved like a merman from a single chunk of apricot jade. In a third he discovered a chess set with diamond and ruby pieces facing each other invitingly, ready for a game. On the walls were portraits of handsome men and women, elegantly dressed in the cloaks and ruffles of a hundred years ago.

By the time the merchant arrived at the dining room he was

exhausted and famished. The table was laid for one, and the most savory odors rose from a roast pheasant on a silver platter.

"I hope the master of this house will pardon me," said the merchant.

Having excused himself to the air, he seized a drumstick and ate heartily. Pumpkin soup with ginger, apple strudel with caramel sauce, wild mushrooms and hot chestnuts and buttered biscuits — he had never eaten a better meal in his life. When he reached for a crystal carafe, he was startled to see it rise of its own accord and fill his goblet with an excellent wine.

"I must be in the house of some good spirit," he exclaimed.

He gazed into the fire. Two andirons shaped like griffins gazed back at him. Over the mantel hung a clock as large and gold as the harvest moon, and while he was admiring it, the clock struck twelve, and a door opened in the far wall to reveal a spacious bedroom. The bed looked so inviting that the merchant pulled off his wet clothes, lay down, and instantly fell asleep.

When he awoke, the morning light was streaming over the silken comforter. Still he saw no one and heard nothing. He reached for his clothes — but what was this? His old suit was clean, dry, and as good as the day he'd bought it in New York — better, in fact, for during the night the plain brass buttons on his jacket had turned to delicate gold medals, incised with stars.

He dressed quickly and was delighted to find an excellent breakfast awaiting him. Especially delicious was the hot chocolate in a silver pot identical to one he had sold a few months before.

Suddenly he remembered poor Blackett, and wiping the chocolate from his mouth, he hurried to the front door. It sprang open before the merchant could touch it, and he stepped out on the broad veranda. Was the frightful blizzard of yesterday a dream? Before him lay a garden fragrant with the brilliant flowers of summer, all blooming at once: peonies and marigolds and lilies with curled petals, crimson poppies and lavender blue delphiniums. And beyond the garden stretched a lawn like a field of tender emeralds that rolled down, down, past a gazebo and a stable and a greenhouse to an inlet of dark blue water.

And—oh joy!—here was Blackett on the lawn, his nose plunged into a bowl of fresh oats.

The merchant seized Blackett's reins and set out for the road. As he was walking his horse along one of the garden paths, he passed an arcade of trellises on which grew an avalanche of red roses. Their fragrance overpowered him; their thorns caught at his sleeve and tugged at his memory.

He stretched out his hand and picked a single perfect rose.

Instantly a howl shook the peace of the garden, and into his path sprang a beast so hideous that the merchant would gladly have faced ten blizzards to escape with his life. Neither dragon nor basilisk, griffin nor winged serpent stood before him, but a creature altogether unfamiliar, tall as a man, who walked on two legs and wore a tuxedo with white waistcoat and tails, such as the merchant himself once wore to balls and dinners before he lost his fortune.

"Ungrateful man!" roared the Beast. "I saved your life, and you steal my roses, which I love more than anything in the world. For this you shall die."

26

The merchant dropped the reins and sank to his knees. He was trembling so hard he could scarcely speak.

"Oh, your honor —"

"Don't flatter me. I'm not a judge. You can see for yourself I am a Beast."

"Oh, my Lord Beast," whimpered the merchant, "I didn't pick the rose —"

"What is that flower in your hand?"

"It's true, I did pick it, but not for myself."

"For whom, then?"

"For my daughter," whispered the merchant.

The Beast seemed to look past him at something very interesting on the horizon.

"You have a daughter?" he inquired in a softer voice.

"Three," said the merchant.

So deep a silence fell between them the merchant heard nothing but the Beast's breath and the chattering of his own teeth.

"Send me one of your daughters to die in your place, and I'll set you free. You can rest assured that if your daughter does not come to me tomorrow morning, you will meet a terrible death in the woods."

"Dear Lord Beast —"

"Out of my sight!"

The merchant looked this way and that but saw no trace of Blackett.

"Since your horse has run off," said the Beast, "I shall give you the loan of mine."

Down the path toward him trotted a magnificent white steed. From its jeweled saddle hung several leather bags, packed, he supposed, with food and water. Scarcely had the merchant settled himself on the horse's back than it took off at enormous speed, flying over broken branches and fallen trees. His breath froze in the air, his fingers felt numb, he was riding back into winter. But where the storm had raged, the sun was now making a harvest of jewels on the sun-tipped spikes of the spruces, and every branch of every tree glittered in a full suit of crystal armor.

As he galloped across the frozen fields, he spied his three daughters running toward him.

"Papa!" cried Vanessa. "We were so worried! When Blackett came home without you, we thought you'd frozen to death in the blizzard!"

The girls hugged him, took his coat, and urged him toward a seat in front of the fire. But before he'd even shaken the snow from his boots, Mona asked, "Did you bring us our presents?"

The merchant shook his head. The captain of his ship had cheated him, he said, and they were no richer than before, and if the cloak and the jewels ever arrived, he would have to return them. To Beauty he gave the rose, as fresh as when it was picked, though he'd clutched it in his gloved fist all the way home.

"This is for you, Beauty," he said wearily, "and it will cost me my life."

And he told them how he'd lost his way in the storm and how he'd been forced to strike a terrible bargain with the Beast.

"Oh, Papa, I'm so sorry," whispered Beauty.

Mona and Vanessa turned on Beauty in a rage.

"You could have asked for a diamond rose studded with pearls," shouted Mona, "but, no, you had to be different."

"A new gown, that was too easy, wasn't it?" sneered Vanessa.

Outside the little window, the white horse was pawing the snow and tossing his head. Beauty stood up and put on her shawl.

"I'll unpack the bags and put the Beast's horse in our stable."

The merchant went out to help her, and together they unbuckled the three saddlebags.

"At least he has sent us some provisions," said Beauty.

But good heavens! The bags were so heavy they could hardly hold them.

"What can be in them?" asked the merchant.

Beauty opened one and gave a cry, and the magnificent white horse turned and galloped across the fields into the forest. Instead of food and drink, the bags were crammed with gold coins, rubies, sapphires, pearls, and, yes, a diamond tiara, an emerald necklace, and a fur-lined cloak.

Together Beauty and her father hauled the bags into the house. *Clink clitter,* chimed the jewels as Vanessa sat by the fireplace and sifted them through her fingers. *Clank chinkle,* sang the coins as Mona counted and recounted them and arranged them into neat piles on the floor. At the bottom of the biggest bag was a book, *The Language of Flowers.*

"This must be for you, Beauty," said Vanessa.

"It's glorious to be rich again," sang Mona.

Tears were rolling down the merchant's cheeks.

"Tomorrow the Beast will devour me, and all you two can think of is being rich."

Beauty put her arms around him.

"No, he won't, Papa. Since I'm the cause of the trouble, I'm the one who should go."

The merchant absolutely would not agree to that. Mona suggested that with all their new money, they could hire someone to shoot the Beast. But the merchant looked grave and shook his head.

"Don't think it's so easy to kill him. His power is far too great."

They went to bed at last, having decided nothing. Mona and Vanessa were soon asleep, and the merchant, who did not think he could close his eyes for worrying, also fell into a deep slumber. Beauty got out of bed, dressed herself in her best blouse and jumper, and brought up one of the saddlebags. But while she was putting her books and clothes into it, she asked herself, "What need do I have of these things if the Beast is going to eat me?"

So she unpacked her clothes but could not bear to leave behind the five books that had belonged to her mother, and into the bag went the books. As she crept down the ladder from the loft, she heard her sisters snoring away with not a care in the world, and she hated them for it.

Downstairs she tiptoed into the living room and knelt by her father's bed and wanted to hug him; he looked so much smaller and thinner than when he was sitting by the fireplace. No, it was better not to wake him. She leaned over and kissed him. Then she put on her shawl and her boots and her mittens and took the rose from the table; it was still fresh.

"I'll take Blackett as far as the Beast's house," she told herself. "He knows the way home."

As she headed toward the barn, she was astonished to see the magnificent white horse waiting in front of the door.

"Your master keeps his promises," said Beauty. She buckled the bag into place and swung herself into the saddle and took hold of the reins. Instantly the horse broke into a gallop across the fields. It seemed no time at all before they were in the woods.

The air grew warm. New leaves misted the maples and shagbark hickories. In this part of the forest the snow was gone, and now the bees hummed, and the creamy plumes of the chestnuts gave off a soapy smell. They passed through a clearing, rich with wild strawberries so juicy that the horse's hooves seemed to be dripping blood.

Ahead of her, cypresses swayed like dark flames. The white horse quickened its pace through the forest. Beauty felt her own heart quicken. The fragrant chill of spruces surrounded her, then the woods opened into another clearing. At the end of the road loomed a tall, dark house that both terrified and enchanted her. The horse trotted up to the front steps and stopped as if to say, "This is as far as I go. You must find your own way from here."

She dismounted and tiptoed up the steps to the veranda, which wound all around the house.

Beauty would gladly have sat down on the steps, for she was in no hurry to enter. Life had never seemed sweeter than at this moment when she was about to lose it, but what use was regret now?

She reached for the door knocker. It had the shape of a winged serpent, which stared at her with ruby eyes.

"I wonder if it can see me?"

Before she could knock, the door opened by itself, slowly and dreamily. Beauty stepped over the threshold. Dazzled by the sunlight, she could see nothing. Then little by little, the house revealed itself.

Twined around the newel post, a silver dragon was clasping a lantern cut from a single diamond that spangled the long corridor before her with brilliant pawprints of light. To her left, a wide staircase wound up and up, past streams of rose and amber light falling through the stained-glass windows.

Beauty tiptoed down the corridor and entered the first room. A soft glow surrounded the chairs and cabinets, the tables and dishes; everything in the room was made of pearl. She saw none of the rarities her father had seen, for the Beast's house never showed the same sights to different people. On one wall glittered a painting of the sea, and as Beauty paused to admire it, she heard the hum of a thousand seashells. This so unsettled her that she hurried into the second room, where a dozen golden chairs were drawn up in a circle. Each chair was upholstered in feathers of the thinnest silver, and when Beauty paused to stroke the feathers, the chairs began to sing:

> "Apple, orange, lemon, lime.
> Lady from the town of time,

Count the pages of your dreams.
Nothing here is as it seems."

She fled from the singing chairs and passed through room after room, each more splendid than the last, but Beauty thought only of the Beast. In what room was he lurking? Did he know a young girl was lost in his house?

The smell of food quickened her step to the dining room, where a friendly fire crackled in the fireplace. Peering through the flames, the matched griffins regarded her gravely. The moonfaced clock on the mantel ticked and tocked. Beauty spied a chessboard on a low table near the fire, the diamond and ruby pieces set up for a game. The diamond pieces looked like her father's at home, but the ruby pieces — ah, how different! The king was a lion, the queen a tiger, the knights unicorns, the castles snails, the pawns monkeys.

Best of all was the long table set with a feast fit for a queen. There were pecan scones and buttercakes, there was roast goose and fresh bread and honeyed carrots, a bowl of ice cream and a silver platter laden with gingerbread dragons frosted in chocolate. Lemonade glittered in an amethyst pitcher held aloft by an airy hand so delicate it seemed etched on the air.

Her hunger was now greater than her fear, so she sat down at the table and ate heartily. The airy hand pressed her to take another slice of goose, another gingerbread dragon. Beauty took seconds of everything and made the meal last as long as she could. But when the last bite of ice cream was gone, the clock struck seven, and she heard such a snorting and a roaring that she gripped the arms of her chair and prepared for the worst.

Then the Beast loped into the room.

E WAS THE MOST MONstrous creature she had ever seen. Her knees were knocking, and she could scarcely stand to meet him, but she was determined not to let the Beast see her fear, even when he eyed her all over, as if he were deciding how to eat this delicate morsel.

"Did you come of your own free will?" he asked.

"Yes, Beast," answered Beauty with a shudder.

"I'm delighted to hear it," remarked the Beast. "You are a brave girl."

This was such a polite response that Beauty's hopes rose. Evidently satisfied with her reply, the Beast turned and trotted out of the room.

Beauty sank into her chair, so relieved that she almost laughed.

"At least he doesn't mean to eat me right away," she told herself.

All at once she heard a loud *hisssssss* in another wing of the house, and her courage melted. She put her face in her hands and cried. Instantly the hissing ceased. From far off came the singing of birds in the garden. Beauty lifted her head.

"What good are tears if I'm about to be eaten?" she whispered.

No sooner had she dried her eyes than she noticed a blue door studded with gold stars, on which was written in letters of gold:

BEAUTY'S APARTMENT

As if it had been waiting to catch her attention, the door swung open. Beauty stepped inside and gave a cry of pleasure. Here was the room she had wanted all her life. A laurel tree grew in the center, its crown reaching through the skylight to the sun. Pots of roses and lilies of the valley perfumed the air, and a fountain hidden in a basin of ferns welcomed her with the most joyful music that seemed to wind in and out between the bed, the piano, the desk, the dressing table.

First she sat down at the piano and played a few chords, then she stretched out on the bed, which was heaped with crimson comforters, then she sat down at the desk and opened the little drawers and was delighted to find a golden pen, bottles of ink in every color, and sketchbooks bound in velvet and embroidered with her name. She opened the closet and saw it was filled with comfortable dresses and one dress of apricot satin that did not look comfortable but was very beautiful. In a crystal vase on the bureau stood the rose her father had picked, and on the table by her bed, her mother's books, a mirror in a jeweled frame, and a diamond cut like a star, which lit the whole room.

At the foot of the bed lay the bag she had brought with her. Empty.

Beauty picked up the mirror, and a sweet voice sang:

> "Welcome, Beauty, have no fear.
> You are queen and mistress here.
> Winter's night is summer's day.
> Speak your wishes, I obey."

"I want to see my father, please," said Beauty. "I'm sure my leaving has been very hard on him."

A spindle of light quivered in the mirror, and Beauty held her breath. Her father's image was taking shape there, and now she saw him seated at the fireplace, staring into the flames, tears running down his face. Behind him, Mona was shelling peas and eating them as she worked. Vanessa swept the kitchen and sang. Beauty was shocked; her sisters did not appear to miss her at all.

In the next instant the scene disappeared, and a door at the far end of her bedroom opened. Beauty turned from the mirror and stepped into her own library, with ladders for reaching the high shelves and a globe of the moon on a three-legged stand and a comfortable chair of green leather. She ran her eye eagerly along the titles and was delighted to find books on magic and mythology and music and poetry.

"The Beast certainly doesn't want me to be bored," exclaimed Beauty. A hopeful thought came to her: "If the Beast intended to eat me, he would not have given me all these comforts."

First she took down a thin volume, which she recognized as the one the Beast had sent her: *The Language of Flowers.* She had not read it then. Now she was delighted to find it contained the names of flowers and what they meant:

Enchanter's Nightshade — Witchcraft

White Rose — I am worthy of you.

Red Carnation — Alas for my poor heart!

Next she picked up a book titled *People with Paws, Claws, Wings, Stings, and Others without Either,* and she curled up in the green leather chair and was soon so lost in the stories that she did not realize the day had slipped away until a bell interrupted her.

She put down her book and listened; was someone singing? Was there another human being here? Beauty followed the music to the dining room and was pleased to find a good supper set for her. Harps and flutes sweetened the air with song, yet there were neither instruments nor musicians to be seen, though Beauty recognized the voices of the golden chairs, who sang with great feeling from the next room.

"A beautiful girl rides into the woods.
The fox would save her if he could.
The bear and badger mean no harm,
And the falcon rests on her outstretched arm.
She finds a mansion, dark and grand.
The door unlocks at her command.
She finds a staircase, high and wide.
The shadows skip and glimmer and glide.
She finds a table laid for one,
With custard tarts and a cinnamon bun.
Rings for her fingers and pearls for her hair,
But who's that growling behind her chair?"

She seated herself at the table and lifted her fork and was about to take a bite of savory meat pie when she heard footsteps padding behind her and a low hiss that turned her blood to ice.

"Beauty," said the monster, "would you allow me to watch you eat your supper?"

"What can I say?" stammered Beauty. "You are the master here."

"No," said the Beast. "It is you who are the mistress of this house. If I annoy you, you have only to tell me, and I shall go away at once."

Though Beauty did not dare ask him to leave, she felt certain that he was not going to eat her tonight. The Beast came forward and leaned against the mantelpiece and fixed his gaze on her.

"Do you find me very ugly?" he asked.

"I can't lie to you," said Beauty. "I do find you ugly." At this, the

Beast looked so crestfallen that she hastened to add, "But I also think you are very kind."

"Oh, I am, I am," exclaimed the monster. "And I have a good heart, Beauty. What a pity I'm so stupid."

"You aren't stupid if you think you are," said Beauty.

The Beast wagged his head from side to side as Beauty had seen the bear do in the woods at home, and it gave her a queer feeling in the pit of her stomach.

"Enjoy your supper, Beauty," said the Beast, "and try to be happy in this house. Everything in it is yours."

"Won't you have some meat pie?" she asked, hoping to direct his appetite toward something besides herself.

"No, thank you. I've already had my supper."

Beauty did not like to think about what he might have eaten for supper; she thanked her stars that it was not herself. He was watching her through eyes narrowed to slits; if he had not been leaning against the mantelpiece, she would have thought he was asleep. But when she went to sit by the fire, his eyes widened ever so slightly. He was watching, watching.

And now Beauty's gaze fell on the chess pieces, sparkling in the firelight.

"Would you like to play?" asked Beauty, and she pointed to the pieces.

"I would love to, if only I weren't such a stupid Beast."

"Let me teach you the game," said Beauty. "I do so want some-one to play with."

They drew up chairs before the little table. Beauty explained

41

the moves, and the Beast learned them so easily that she wondered if he already knew them and had simply forgotten them. Or perhaps he was only pretending he didn't know, so that he could enjoy her company without alarming her. She tried not to show her horror as his claws groped for his pieces, and she had to help him make his moves.

"Fingers," sighed the Beast. "There's nothing in the whole world quite like fingers."

The fire was beginning to make her feel sleepy, and she let herself believe that the Beast meant her no harm.

"You've done very well for your first time," she said. "Shall we finish the game tomorrow?"

"Beauty — ," said the Beast.

Something in his voice made her uneasy. At his next words, terror seized her.

"Beauty, will you be my wife?"

She did not dare to reply at once, for fear her refusal would madden him.

"No, Beast," she said at last.

His sigh, half howl and half hiss, echoed all over the house.

"I hope you'll allow me to ask you again another night," he said. "Farewell, Beauty." He turned to look back at her again and again before he closed the door and vanished from her sight.

That night before she fell asleep under the crimson comforter, she remembered the Beast's paw pushing his king forward, as

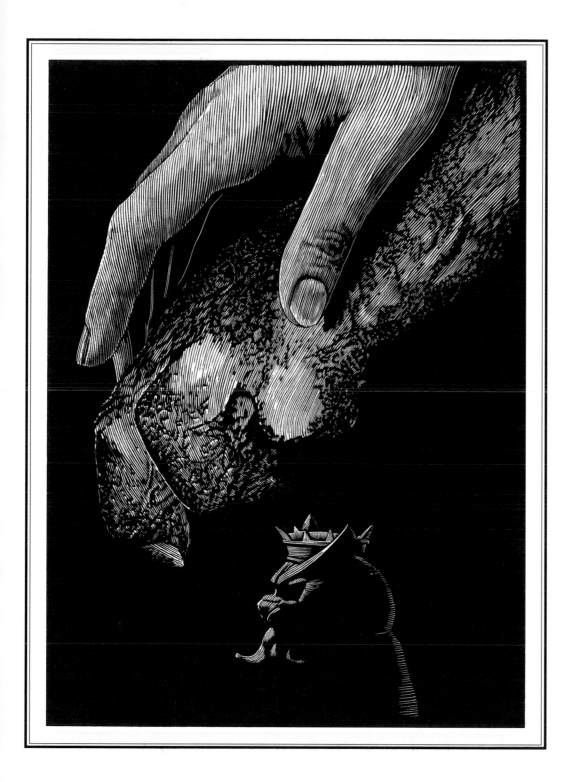

clumsy as a bandaged hand, and she felt so sorry for him that her eyes filled with tears.

"He's not as fierce as I thought," she thought, "but I shall certainly have nightmares about those claws."

But she did not have nightmares. No, indeed. She dreamed that her mother was bending over her, whispering into her ear, "I'm proud of you, my girl. Nothing is as it seems, is it? You take after me."

The next morning Beauty woke to find toast and jam in a basket and hot chocolate in a midnight-blue pot studded with stars waiting for her on her dressing table. She looked for her old blouse and jumper, which she had hung in the closet, and discovered they were as new as the day she'd first put them on — and much prettier, for in the night they had embroidered themselves with red roses that had the fragrance of real ones. Beauty dressed and ate breakfast quickly.

"It's a grand day to go exploring," she said to herself.

First she examined everything on the veranda, the wicker chairs and the silver pots a-bloom with tulips and daffodils and red carnations. Then she walked all around the house and discovered not just one garden but four, separated by boxwood hedges trimmed in the shapes of a bear, a bobcat, a wolf, and a boar. There were beds of peonies and poppies, bleeding hearts and sweet william, and a brake of ferns in the center of each garden, from which a hidden fountain sang. There was an apple orchard and a grove of orange trees that dropped their golden fruit into her hand.

Beauty had learned a good deal about gardening from her mother's books, and she was puzzled to see snowdrops and crocuses, the first flowers of spring, blooming alongside asters and chrysanthemums, which never appeared before late summer. Rounding a corner, she came upon an arcade of rose bushes, arch opening into arch like a tunnel of fragrant rubies, and a voice in her heart murmured, "Here is where your father picked the fateful rose." At once she wished she could be home with him, though the same voice said sternly, "You are a great deal more comfortable in the Beast's house than you were at home waiting on your sisters."

At the edge of the gardens grew a grove of white birches, through which the river sparkled. But the air here felt chilly and strange. As she turned to go back, she caught sight of a tower on the west wing of the house, its round panes a curve of gold in the late afternoon sun.

Nothing cures homesickness quicker than an unexplored tower.

She ran back along the path to the house. Instead of returning to her own room, she followed the stairs, which wound under the light pouring through the amber and rose windows.

In the first window over the stairs glittered the portrait of a young man with red hair and a red beard, walking the garden that Beauty had just left. He wore muddy boots and a jacket and carried a silver trowel.

"He must be the gardener," thought Beauty. Had the Beast eaten him?

In the second window the same young man, now wearing a tuxedo, was seated at the chessboard in the dining room.

"Well, he's certainly not the gardener," said Beauty to herself and longed to meet him, for the light winking across his face made it appear he was about to tell a very funny joke.

The third window showed him gazing into a starry sky. On his lap lay a map of the heavens. The young man looked so lifelike that when she whispered, "Did you live in this house once?" she half expected him to answer, "Of course."

At the top of the stairs lay a long corridor, and as Beauty followed it past room after room, she heard the joyful song of water, as if a secret spring were bubbling through the house. She peered into first one room, then another, and was astonished to find that each had its own fountain, in which goldfinches chirped and splashed.

"How nice for the birds — they don't live in cages," she remarked and wondered if the door at the end of the corridor would show her a way out of the Beast's house. The door opened on a flight of smaller stairs, much higher and narrower than the others. These she climbed to a vast dark room.

"Nothing here," she said, and then as her eyes grew used to the dark, she was astonished at what she saw. There were toboggans and teddy bears, sleds and ski poles, books and bicycles and bolts of creamy satin, a globe and a gramophone, and a steamer trunk out of which spilled plumed hats, velvet capes, and yards of lace. There was a ship in a bottle and a pair of russet slippers spangled with pearls. Strangest of all were the shadows on the walls, for they did not look a bit like the objects around her but took the shapes of men and women dancing, bearing trays, and lighting lamps. She thought of the shadow people her father's butler had shown her and her sisters in the old house on Fifth Avenue, before her father lost his fortune. But no one she could see was making these shadows.

"I shall get to the bottom of this," she exclaimed.

Against one wall leaned a huge oil painting of a child in his nightgown peering out from a crowd of beasts both friendly and wild. The brass plate on the golden frame read: *The Peaceable Kingdom.*

Most intriguing of all was the photograph album lying on the floor.

Beauty picked up the album, leafed through it, and recognized the young man from the windows over the stairs, though in many of the pictures he was much younger. In one he was playing with a large black dog. In another he was taking tea with his parents in the gazebo; on the back someone had written: *William, age 14.* In a third picture William was riding the horse that had brought Beauty here. At the bottom, she could just make out the words: *William and his horse, Hesperides.*

"What a pity William has moved away," she said to herself. "I'd love to have someone I could talk to, besides the Beast."

A photograph dropped from the book into her hand. It showed William kneeling in a round bright room. She turned the picture over and was surprised to find a small reproduction of *The Peaceable Kingdom* taped to the back.

"Odd," said Beauty and puzzled over it. Then an idea came to her, and she pushed the painting aside and was overjoyed to see that it hid another flight of stairs. These were so steep she had to go up on hands and knees, but when she clambered out into the light, she found herself in the tower at last.

It was a wonderful room, as round as a drum, with curved windows even taller than her father, and window seats under them. The marble fountain in the center of the room sparkled and sang more beautifully than all the others, though no birds splashed here. She tried the windows, and they opened easily — why, she could step right out on the roof!

The wind blew her hair as she planted her feet on the flat roof on the back of the Beast's house and gazed about her. To the east, she recognized the gazebo and the stables; a weathervane like a winged horse was spinning on the cupola. Beyond the stables, Hesperides grazed in the greenest of pastures.

"Maybe I can see our cottage," she said and wondered what her father and her sisters were doing at that moment.

No, she couldn't see that far. But beyond the Beast's gardens, trees bowed to each other under the weight of fresh snow, and ice cutters worked on the frozen river. Her head was spinning; she felt as if she were standing in two seasons at once and might fall into the crack between winter and spring.

Hastily she climbed down into the tower room again.

The day had passed so quickly that she could hardly believe dinner was less than an hour away. For the first time since she arrived, she wanted to wear the gown of apricot satin that hung in the closet. She slipped it on, and the back buttons fastened themselves, for which she was grateful, since she did not wish to be late for the Beast.

At seven o'clock he appeared and leaned against the mantel-piece and watched her eat, as before.

"I hope you are not bored," he said.

No, she wasn't. She told him how much she admired his gardens, but she did not mention the tower.

"Even a monster can love flowers," said the Beast.

"Many folks with handsome faces are greater monsters than you," said Beauty. "Their ugliness is all inside them."

"Do you think you can be happy here, Beauty? Is there anything you want that you don't have?"

The way he asked it reminded her of her father's question: *Beauty, what can I bring back for you? There must be something you want.* She could not think of a thing, but she did not want to disappoint the Beast.

"I wish I had a little rose garden of my own," she said. "Your roses are beautiful, but they don't need anyone to tend them."

The next morning she took the path to the gazebo and was surprised to discover a silver trowel and a lunch pail. Beside the gazebo a tangle of thyme, rosemary, and everlasting grew around a weedy bed of wild roses. Beauty set to work, pruning and pulling. When she glanced up, the sun was glinting in the tower window, and she thought she saw a face — the Beast's, perhaps, but she was not sure. What, she wondered, did he do all day? And how long did he mean to keep her? To stay here for years and years and never see anyone but the Beast — ah, that would be horrible. She would die of unhappiness in this place where everything was provided for her happiness.

The shadows of the trees stretched like lazy cats in the afternoon sun. Beauty had forgotten to eat her lunch, and it would soon be time to meet the Beast for dinner; she gathered up her lunch pail and trowel. Suddenly a thorn from the roses raked her hand and opened a bloody seam along her knuckles.

She searched her pockets for her handkerchief, but before she could locate it, something crashed in the underbrush behind her, and she spun around to see the Beast lumbering toward her.

"This will stop the bleeding," he said, "and take away the pain."

He looked as wild as if he had been chasing small animals through the forest. Beauty was terribly frightened until he uncurled his claws and showed her the leaves he had brought her. She extended her bloody hand and let him lay them over the cut. When he put her hand to his mouth she thought, "So he means to eat me after all," but she did not run away — what good would it do? And when he licked the leaves into place with his rough tongue, she did not know whether to laugh or cry. The blood stopped, and the pain vanished, just as he promised.

"You've made my hand well again," she said. "Thank you."

"The forest is full of heal-all," he said. "Beauty, will you dine with me in the garden?"

This delighted her; it was a change from their usual evening ritual.

The supper arranged itself in the gazebo, and Beauty ate while the Beast watched. She asked him about the flowers and herbs that grew on his land, and he told her their names and uses.

"You know a great deal about flowers," she exclaimed.

"I know only what a Beast would know," he said. "Beauty, will you marry me?"

Beauty put down her fork in despair.

"Oh no, Beast."

That night she could not fall asleep. The laurel leaves rustled overhead. Beauty thought of the Beast licking the pain out of her hand, she thought of the young man in the glass windows and the photo album, she thought of the little round room at the top of the house. The sky would be thick with stars — and here she was, wide awake, and missing the splendor.

She climbed out of bed and listened at the doorway of her room for the Beast. Hearing nothing more than the musical rise and fall of fountains singing throughout the house, she picked up the diamond star that lit her room, cupped her fingers around it, and ran through the house till she reached the stairs. If she met the Beast, would he think she was running away? She did not like to think what would happen to her if he caught her.

The stained-glass windows were dark, the handsome young man invisible. Down the corridor she sped, up the stairs to the attic, running and climbing till she came to the tower.

How different the tower room looked by night! It was as if someone had wrapped the windows in stars. She knelt on the window seat and searched for the Big Dipper. Her mother had called it Ursa Major, the Great Bear. Ah, if only she'd paid attention when her mother tried to teach her about the stars!

Her father would be sleeping now, with the starlight falling on him through the little window in the living room.

"If I could peep into that room and get a glimpse of him, just for a moment."

Beauty was so absorbed in the sky that she did not hear the door open, only the soft growl of the Beast, which made her heart nearly stop beating. She was trapped.

"If I'm annoying you," said the Beast meekly, "I shall go away."

The gentleness of his voice calmed her.

"You often startle me," Beauty said, "but you never annoy me."

The Beast made a pleased, purring sound.

"I often come here, to look at the heavenly beasts," he said. "Such faithful friends they are, the beasts."

And he lifted his paw and showed her the bright beasts shining in the sky: the dragon, the dog, the swan, the snake, the winged horse, the bull, the crab, reeling and wheeling their way toward morning.

Suddenly his voice cracked.

"Beauty, will you marry me?"

"Oh, Beast, I wish you wouldn't keep asking. Let me be your friend. Can you be happy with that?"

The Beast was silent for a long time.

"Beauty," he said at last, "promise me one thing. Never leave me."

By the light of the heavenly beasts in the starlit tower, she could not see how ugly he looked, and it was easy for her to say yes.

ONTHS PASSED, AND
Beauty refrained from asking the magic mirror about life in the cottage, for she knew it would make her homesick to see the little house roofed in snow, and the bare orchard, and Blackett dozing in the barn, and her father sitting by the fire. From the roof of the Beast's house, she liked to watch the ice choppers pushing their way up and down the river, and the woods beyond his lands, broken and bowed with snow. "If my father were not all right, I would have heard," she assured herself.

When she played the piano in her room, she had the feeling that the Beast was listening, though she never saw him except in the evening. And while she was reading in her library, or walking in the gardens, she found herself dreaming of what she would wear and what they would say to each other. Sometimes she picked an apple and strolled down to the stable to visit Hesperides. She never rode him anymore, for he obeyed only the Beast, but she always shared her apple with him when they ambled together in the fragrant pastures beyond the stable.

At seven o'clock the Beast appeared. Since he was all the com-

pany she had, Beauty greatly looked forward to his coming. After she'd eaten her dinner she would read him a fairy tale from one of her mother's books, and he would tell her about the wind and how it looks like bright scarves to animals who have the gift of seeing it.

"The streams running through my woods carry the dreams of the animals that drink there. Their dreams make the water taste sweet."

Or they would play a game of chess in the gazebo, and Beauty would help him move the pieces.

When darkness fell, Beauty would say, "Let's visit the stars," and the Beast followed her obediently to the tower, where they sat together on the window seat and scanned the sky, and he told her how the wild geese flying south sing to the stars, and she wondered how she could ever have been afraid of him.

And when Beauty said, "You know so many interesting things," he would say, "I only know what a Beast knows." And after a pause: "Beauty, will you marry me?"

"Beast, I am sorry. My answer will always be the same."

She wanted very much to ask him about the gentleman in the windows and the photographs, but whenever she passed through the attic with the Beast, all the treasures, including the album, disappeared, and Beauty took this as a sign she should not mention him.

One morning as she looked out across the valley from the tower, she noticed a green veil on the tops of trees that had once been swathed in snow.

"I've been with the Beast for the whole winter," she told herself. "Surely I can see my father now, without feeling homesick."

And she went straight to her room, seized the magic mirror, and said, "I want to see my father."

Immediately his image appeared in the glass. But how changed! Alone, sick, he lay shivering in his bed by the fireplace. The fire had gone out, and the cupboards were bare.

"Why is my father alone?" cried Beauty.

His face faded, and the mirror showed her Vanessa and Mona with their new husbands riding together in a smart carriage through Central Park. Though Beauty could not hear their words, it was clear they were having an argument. Suddenly Mona pushed one of the young men out of the carriage, and the other man seized the chance to escape and jumped out also. Vanessa struck Mona with her fan, and the driver of the carriage stopped and ordered them to pay their fare; he would carry them no farther.

Then the image vanished. Beauty threw herself on her bed and wept. Seven o'clock came and went, but Beauty did not go to dinner. Presently she heard the Beast's padding footfall outside her room and the queer scraping his claws made when he knocked at her door.

"Beauty, are you ill?"

"Yes, Beast," sobbed Beauty.

The door opened and he shambled in, and Beauty climbed out of her bed and threw herself at his feet.

"My father is sick. Please, won't you let me go home, just for a week?"

The Beast knelt and raised her and kept one paw on her arm. He was silent for such a long time that Beauty was afraid she had angered him.

"I can't bear to see you unhappy," he said in a voice as small as a cricket's. "So I'll send you to your father. And you'll stay with him. And your poor Beast will die of grief."

"What nonsense," said Beauty. "I would never do anything to cause your death. I give you my promise: I'll return in a week. Will you let me go?"

Again the Beast did not answer for a long time.

"Tomorrow morning," he said at last, "you'll wake in your father's house. I shall give you a wreath, Beauty. You have only to lay it on your pillow and wish yourself home before you fall asleep. Farewell, Beauty. Remember your promise."

Beauty could not contain her joy.

"I'll remember, I'll remember!"

"Shall we watch the stars one last time before you go?"

"The sky is cloudy," said Beauty. "The beasts are hiding. When I come back we'll watch them. Good night, dear Beast."

Later she scolded herself for this thin excuse. The sky was never cloudy over the Beast's house, but Beauty was too excited to think of anything but her visit home. There on her pillow lay the wreath, woven of everlasting and forget-me-nots and sweet bay and deep red carnations. Beauty took *The Language of Flowers* from her library and looked up the meaning of sweet bay: *I die if neglected*.

She read no further but climbed into bed at once. The wreath

was so fragrant Beauty said to herself, "I shall dream I've fallen asleep in the woods." But she did not dream of the woods. No, indeed. She dreamed her mother was bending over her, whispering in her ear, "Keep your promise, Beauty. If you fail to keep it, you will kill the Beast who loves you."

When Beauty awoke, she found herself on the threshold of the cottage. She pushed open the door. Her father was asleep in his bed by the hearth, and when Beauty rushed forward and kissed him, he whispered, "Am I in heaven, or am I dreaming?"

"Neither," said Beauty. "Papa, I'm home."

When she hugged him, she felt how thin he was. Immediately she set about making the house more comfortable. She fetched water from the well and wood from the shed and lit a fire and made tea for them both, and then she helped her father to his chair and arranged a blanket around his knees while he patted her arm and said, over and over, "I thought you were dead. I thought the Beast had killed you. Every night I dreamed you were dead."

Things had been hard, he added. When Beauty heard he'd sold their faithful Blackett, she could hardly hide her distress.

"What happened to the jewels the Beast sent you before I left?"

"Your sisters took them when they went back to the city to look for husbands. They're nothing but trouble, those two. Mona met a stockbroker, and Vanessa met an admiral."

"Are they living in the city?"

The merchant shook his head.

"They've already quarreled. The girls came home last night in a rage. It's a wonder we didn't wake them."

"Are you telling me my sisters never sent you any money?" cried Beauty.

"Let's forget about them till they wake up," said the merchant. "Tell me about the Beast. Is he kind to you?"

"Oh, he is the kindest Beast in the world," said Beauty.

And she told her father about her room in the Beast's palace, and how thoughtful he was, and how he knew so much about the stars and the flowers and the forest.

"Sometimes I almost forget how ugly he is," said Beauty.

"Do you love the Beast?" asked her father.

"I don't know. I'm very fond of him," said Beauty.

"You're just like your mother, Beauty. You believe in magic."

By noon her sisters were up, and they were astonished to see Beauty and their father laughing and joking together in the living room. Vanessa fingered Beauty's dress and announced that if *she* had an exquisite gown of apricot satin, she would not dirty it with trips to the woodshed.

"Somebody has to fetch the wood," said Beauty.

"Beauty, there's a grand trunk in the loft with your name on it," said Mona. "I can't think how you got it upstairs. But of course you always were as strong as a scullery maid."

"I brought nothing," said Beauty. "The Beast must have sent it."

They all hurried up to the loft. Sure enough, a trunk encrusted with jewels shone in a corner of their dingy bedroom. Beauty opened it, and Vanessa cried, "Oh, what beautiful gowns — dozens of them!" and Mona exclaimed, "Look at the rings and necklaces — they must be worth a fortune."

"Please help yourself," said Beauty.

Instantly the trunk disappeared.

"I think the Beast wants you to keep them, Beauty," said their father.

No sooner had he spoken than the trunk returned.

By the end of the day Mona and Vanessa were acting as if Beauty had never gone away. They waited for Beauty to cook their meals and complained when she served them.

"The soup is too salty!"

"The meat is too hot!"

Every night the larder was empty, and every morning it was full of spiced ham and cheese and oranges and bread. Beauty was glad to see her father gaining strength, and she hated the thought of leaving him in the care of her sisters. He had taught himself to whittle, and he whittled two lambs and a tiny castle out of poplar for Beauty.

"You never made me toys when I was little," she said.

And her father said with a smile, "I can carve almost anything except cats. All my cats look like pigs."

Outside, the crocuses and daffodils she had planted in the fall were sending up soft green tusks. The smell of leaf mold and smoke from wood fires and kettles of boiling sap filled her with excitement. Along the river, their neighbors were making maple sugar and hoping for the first bluebird of the year, whose singing makes the sap run sweeter.

The wild geese were winging north; Beauty heard their joyous honking and thought, "They're singing to the stars." Sunlight flooded the bare forest. The snow was melting, running in bright streams down the hillsides, and Beauty remembered the fountains in the Beast's house. When she drank from the spring, she seemed to be drinking his knowledge: *the dreams of animals make the water sweet.*

"If I could just stay long enough to set my vegetable garden," thought Beauty, and she remembered the herbs she'd tended by the gazebo, where the Beast came to watch her eat and listen to her read stories.

Meanwhile her sisters amused themselves trying on the gowns in the jeweled chest; the Beast seemed to have no objection to their borrowing them.

"It's not fair that Beauty has so many comforts, and we have none," said Vanessa. "If she goes back, we'll have to run the house and take care of Father."

"The Beast won't take her back if she breaks her promise," said Mona. "So let's make sure she breaks her promise."

The week passed quickly. On the last day of Beauty's visit, her sisters got up early, and when Beauty came downstairs Vanessa was making tea.

"Lazybones," she snapped. "You missed the messenger."

"What messenger?" asked Beauty.

"A messenger from the Beast. He says you can stay another week."

"Another week!" exclaimed the merchant, who was listening from the next room. "Ah, Beauty, that news has made me a well man."

And he tottered into the kitchen and sat down at the table, his face radiant. Beauty frowned and turned to Vanessa.

"What did the messenger look like?"

"He had ears like a cat and a tail like a bear, and he wore a purple cloak."

Beauty thought it strange that during her stay at the Beast's house she had never met such a messenger, but she told herself, "Why shouldn't the Beast have a messenger? I know very little about him, really." And she went walking with her father as far as the orchard.

"Listen! Do you hear our woodpecker?" said the merchant.

She nodded, and he took a deep breath.

"I think I have never been happier than I am at this moment," he said.

That night Beauty did not sleep well. By morning the wreath, which she kept under her pillow, was beginning to wilt. When she came downstairs, her father was sipping his tea, and Mona was toasting cheese and bread for one: herself.

"Mona," said Beauty, "did you see the Beast's messenger?"

"Yes, indeed," said Mona, between bites.

"What did he look like?" asked Beauty.

"He had ears like a rabbit and a tail like a snake, and he wore a yellow suit."

"Why, what's the matter, Beauty?" asked her father. "You look terrible."

"I'm sick," said Beauty, and she fled upstairs.

The wreath was nearly dead. Beauty laid it on her pillow, as the Beast had instructed her, and climbed into bed. Sleep did not come; she closed her eyes, she tossed and turned.

"If I don't fall asleep, how can I return to my beloved Beast?" she thought.

She did not remember drifting into sleep, but her closed eyes showed her the Beast stretched out in a pool of moonlight, and the voice in her heart whispered, "He is dying, Beauty."

She woke in her own room, in the Beast's house. She read, she played the piano, she weeded the garden, but she could not make the time pass any faster. At a quarter to seven she put on a white silk gown trimmed with roses and hurried to the dining room to meet the Beast for supper. The fountains were silent, the invisible musicians did not play, and the fire was a heap of embers. Only the clock spoke to her. In seven stern syllables, it struck seven o'clock.

And the Beast did not come.

"Perhaps he's waiting for me in the gazebo," said Beauty.

She ran through all the gardens to the gazebo. There was no sign of the Beast.

Terrified now, she tore through the house and, hiking up the hem of her gown, she took the stairs two at a time, never stopping till she reached the tower. Her heart was pulsing like a drum in her ears as she flung the door open.

On the floor in a pool of moonlight lay the Beast. Beauty threw herself over him and put her ear to his chest and heard, like retreating footsteps, the faint beating of his heart.

"Don't die! Please don't die!"

The Beast's eyelids twitched. The rest of him lay perfectly still. Beauty cupped her hands and scooped water from the fountain and poured it on his head.

"You shall not die, dear Beast," said Beauty. "Live and be my husband. There is no one in the world I love so well as you."

Scarcely had Beauty uttered these words than fireworks lit up the sky. Invisible trumpets blew, and invisible fiddles unleashed a stream of tunes lively enough to set the dead dancing. Bending over the Beast, Beauty was speechless with astonishment when the Beast disappeared and left in his place a young man with red hair and a red beard, who sprang to his feet and bowed to her. He wore muddy boots and a jacket to which clung the fragrance of earth and roses. Beauty recognized him at once. She had gazed at him so often in the windows over the stairs that she knew William's features by heart. He reached for her hand, but she held back.

"Where is my Beast?"

"You see him in front of you," said William.

Now Beauty gave him her hand. Everything in the attic was dancing: the bicycle was dancing with the gramophone, the teddy bears with the toboggans, the ski poles with each other. As they made their way downstairs, she was amazed to behold a bustle of servants, bearing trays of hot dishes, lighting candles in lamps and chandeliers, and greeting each other as after a long absence.

"Where did these people come from?" exclaimed Beauty.

"They were always here," replied William. "They hid in their shadows till the spell on me was lifted."

From the top of the stairs, Beauty spied her father in the front

hall. He was clutching his hat and trying to recover his breath, for he could not imagine what power had carried him to this place.

"Are my sisters here?" asked Beauty.

"Yes, indeed. Follow me," said William.

He led Beauty through the house to the fireplace.

"Look into the flames," said William.

Instead of the matched griffins, Beauty saw her sisters cast in iron and linked by a bar that held up a great many heavy logs.

"I hope the fire does not hurt them," Beauty whispered.

"All that hurts them is the sight of your happiness," said William.

A sweet voice in her ear was singing:

> "Now welcome joy,
> And grief depart.
> To Beast and Bridegroom
> She gave her heart."

And Beauty did not know if the music came from magic or her own heart.

ABOUT THIS BOOK

Newbery Medalist Nancy Willard and American Book Award—winning artist/designer Barry Moser began their collaboration on *Beauty and the Beast* in 1987. Research involved examining existing book versions, including the original story by Madame Leprince Beaumont (1711–1780), as well as film versions, primarily Jean Cocteau's *La Belle et La Bête* (1946). In addition, the writer and illustrator visited Wilderstein in Rhinebeck, New York, one of the Hudson River Valley's oldest homes, which provided many of the written and visual images here. Together Willard and Moser explored the grounds of the estate and the interior of the house you now see on page 33, talking, telling the story back and forth, taking notes, and making photographs. Another outing took them to the Victorian Villa, a house in Union City, Michigan, where Nancy Willard's grandmother was raised.

The illustrations in this book are wood engravings, a relief
printmaking technique. They were engraved in end-grain maple.
The display type and text type were set in Trump Mediaeval
by Thompson Type, San Diego, California.
Color separations were made by Bright Arts, Ltd., Singapore.
Printed and bound by Tien Wah Press, Singapore
Production supervision by Warren Wallerstein and Ginger Boyer
Art Direction by Michael Farmer
Designed by Barry Moser